Housekeeper of the Wind

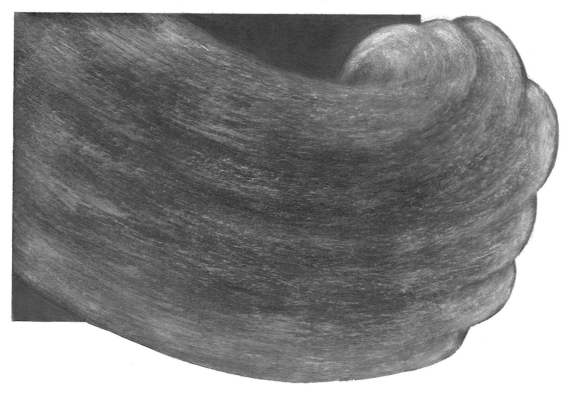

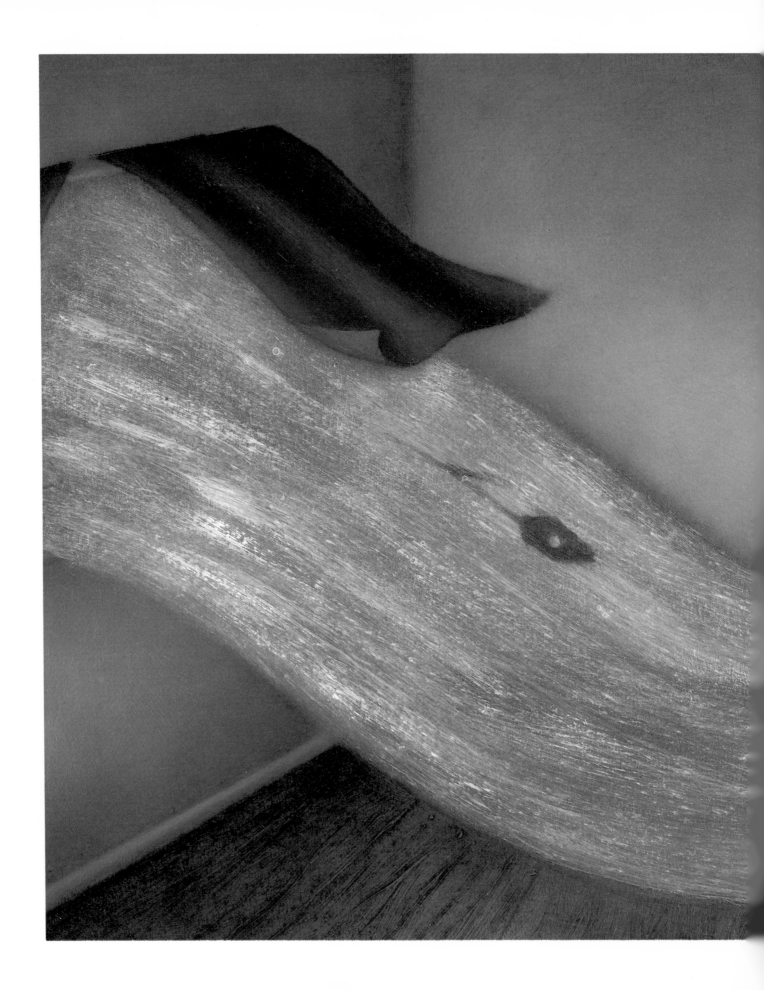

Housekeeper of the Wind

by CHRISTINE WIDMAN

illustrated by LISA DESIMINI

HARPER & ROW, PUBLISHERS

HOUSEKEEPER OF THE WIND

Text copyright © 1990 by Christine Widman
Illustrations copyright © 1990 by Lisa Desimini
All rights reserved. No part of this book may be
used or reproduced in any manner whatsoever without
written permission except in the case of brief quotations
embodied in critical articles and reviews. Printed in
the United States of America. For information address
Harper & Row Junior Books, 10 East 53rd Street,
New York, N.Y. 10022.

Library of Congress Cataloging-in-Publication Data
Widman, Christine.
    Housekeeper of the wind / by Christine Widman ;
illustrated by Lisa Desimini. — 1st ed.
        p.   cm.
    Summary: The wind and his housekeeper become angry with each
other one hot summer day, but apologize with appropriate gifts.
    ISBN 0-06-026467-5 : $ ISBN 0-06-026468-3 (lib. bdg.) : $
    [1. Winds—Fiction.]   I. Desimini, Lisa, ill.   II. Title.
PZ7.W6346Ho 1990   88-10979
[E]—dc19   CIP
                                                              AC

Typography by Elynn Cohen
1   2   3   4   5   6   7   8   9   10
First Edition

ula kept house for the Wind.

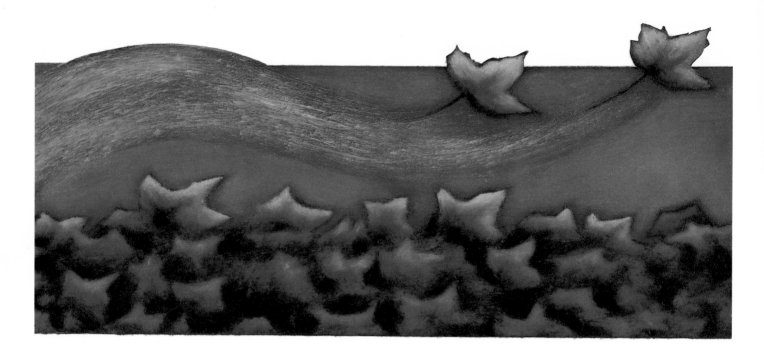

In autumn she swept away crinkled leaves
the Wind brought in after a day of blowing.

In winter she kept a fire glowing in the fireplace
to melt the snowflakes on the Wind's frozen face.

8

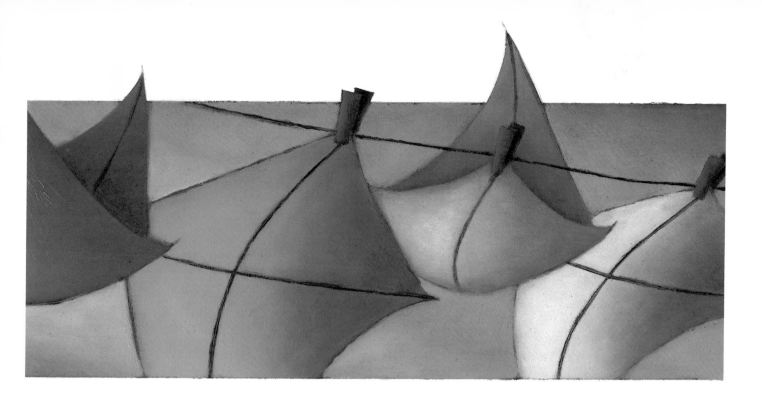

In spring she collected lost kites
the Wind had tossed,
and strung them to a clothesline.

In summer she gathered the fragrance of meadows
the Wind left in the cottage
and put it in bottles to sell at the market.

But one very hot summer day,
the Wind left only the smell of dry grass in the room.
"No one would buy this
to dab behind their ears," complained Yula.
She went outside and lay down on her hammock.
"Wind, blow me a breeze," she said.
The Wind blew,
but its breath was as hot as sand in the sun.
"Go away, Wind! You're no help at all."

The Wind turned to the poplar.
  Whisper rustle
  Whisper rustle
The poplar and the Wind murmured together.
"Be quiet," Yula grumbled.

The Wind turned to the gate.
    Crick creak
    Crick creak
The gate and the Wind swung back and forth together.

14

"Be still!" snapped Yula.
The Wind blew out of the yard and shut the gate.
   BANG
Yula went into the cottage and shut the door.
   SLAM
Yula and the Wind were angry.

The Wind piled black clouds above the cottage
as high as Yula could see.
"Oh dear," sighed Yula. "Wind is brewing up a storm."
"Yuuula, Yuuula," called the Wind down the chimney.
"Blow away," said Yula. "I'm angry with you."
"I'm angry toooo," roared the Wind,
rattling the windows.

Yula covered her ears
and turned her back on the rowdydow Wind.
"I'll make my own hullabaloo!" she hollered.
She grabbed her broom.
    SWISH SWISH SWISH
Yula swept up soot from old campfires
and sand from far shores.
    WHISH WHISH WHISH
Yula swept out fluff from the dandelions
and petals from pansies.
"Look what the Wind blows in on a summer day,"
she muttered.

"Yuuulaaa,"
cried the Wind through a crack in the door.
"Let me in."
"No, Wind!
I've just cleaned house, and you're too wild.

20

You'd gust in the dust and tangle the curtains."
The Wind wailed and pounded rain on the roof,
but Yula didn't listen.
She washed windows instead.

When all her cleaning was done,
Yula opened the door.
No Wind breezed in.
It was quiet outside.
The Wind had stopped storming.
The air was cool.
The Wind had blown away the hot day.
Yula was sorry she'd been angry.
"Oh dear," sighed Yula.
"Wind's gone away in a huff.
 What will bring Wind back?"

She climbed up the stairs into the attic
and opened a trunk marked
   THE WIND'S PLAYTHINGS.
She pulled out wind chimes, a wind sock,
and a kite as blue as the summer sky.
"A kite is just the right thing," said Yula.
She reached back into the trunk
and pulled out six ribbons,
each one as long as a rainbow.
"I'll use these for the kite's tail."

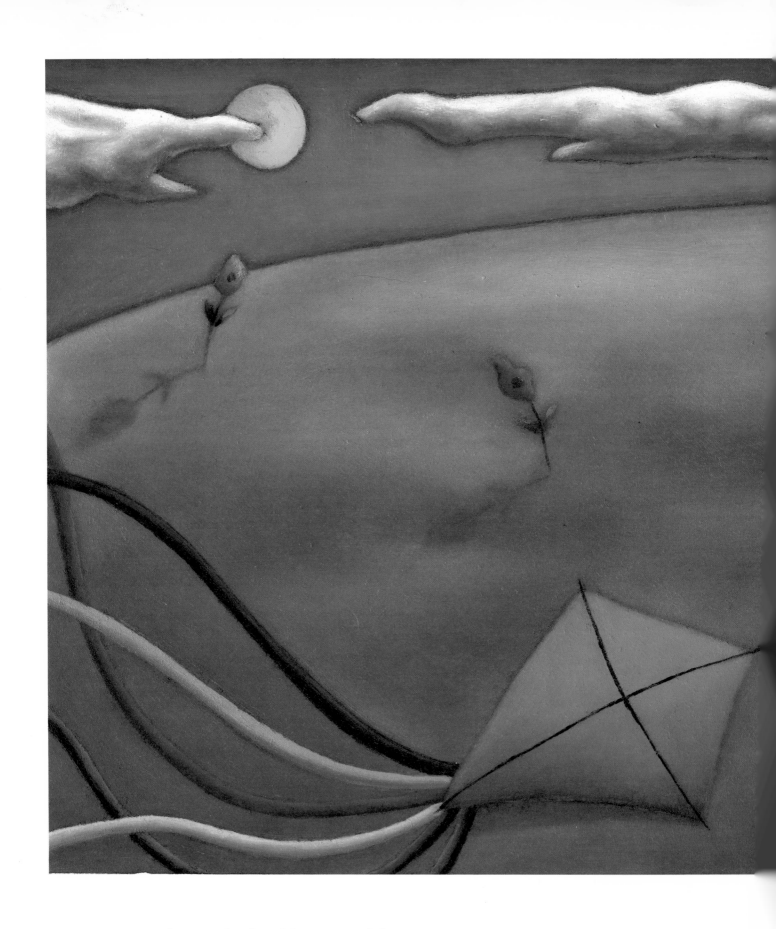

Yula took the kite outside
and ran back and forth with it across the meadow.

26

The kite bumped on the ground behind her.

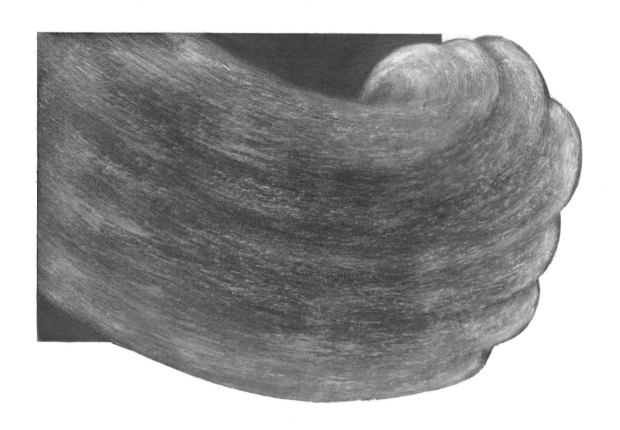

"That won't fly,"
called the Wind from high in the sky.
"I have to try," said Yula.
She set the kite on the fence and began to blow at it.
But only the rainbow tail fluttered.
"That won't gooo," the Wind guffawed.
"Ha ha...ho hoooo."

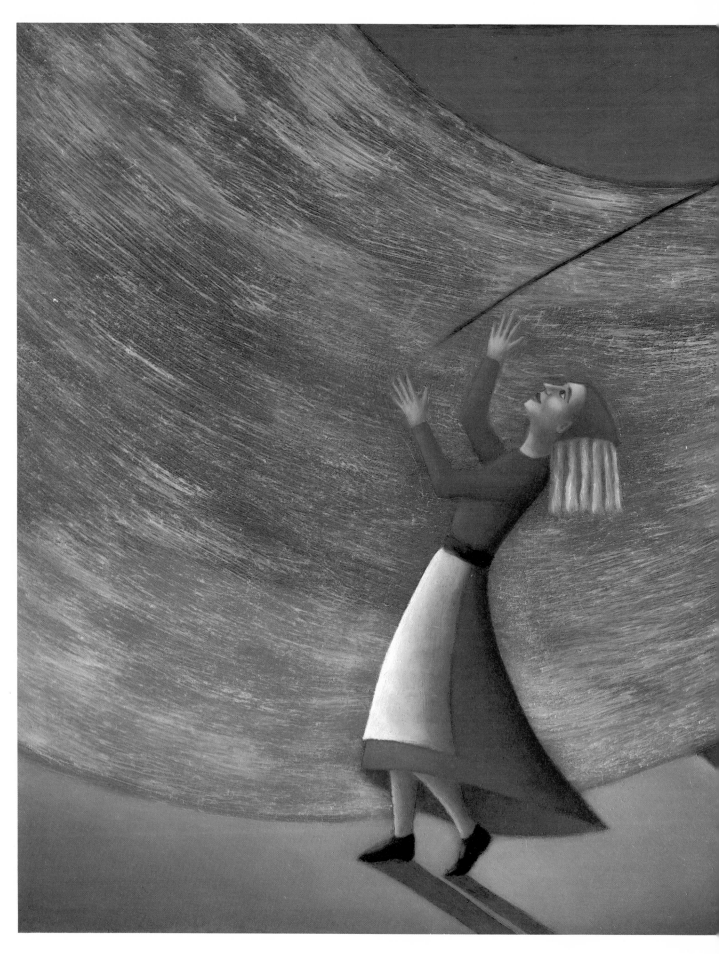

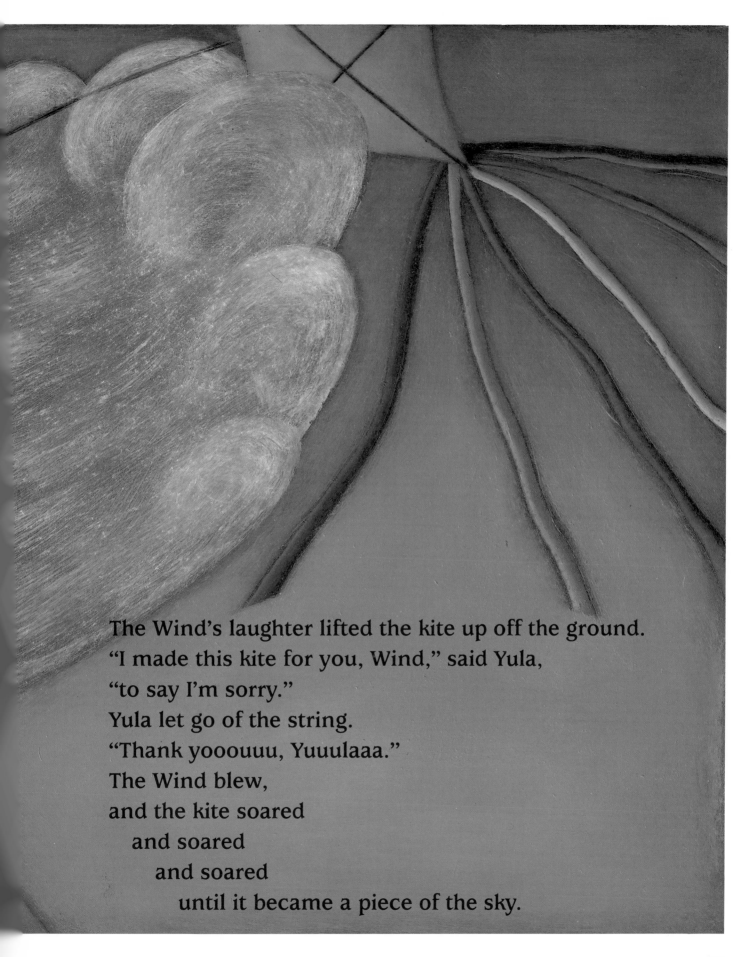

The Wind's laughter lifted the kite up off the ground.
"I made this kite for you, Wind," said Yula,
"to say I'm sorry."
Yula let go of the string.
"Thank yooouuu, Yuuulaaa."
The Wind blew,
and the kite soared
   and soared
      and soared
         until it became a piece of the sky.

Yula walked into the cottage.
The Wind blew in through an open window.
The scent of rain on wild roses filled the room.
The Wind whispered in Yula's ear, "For yoouu."